The Cupcake Tree

Adapted by Gabhi Martins

DreamWorks Gabby's Dollhouse © 2024 DreamWorks Animation LLC. All Rights Reserved.

All rights reserved. Published by Scholastic Inc., *Publishers since 1920*. SCHOLASTIC and associated logos are trademarks and/or registered trademarks of Scholastic Inc.

The publisher does not have any control over and does not assume any responsibility for author or third-party websites or their content.

ISBN 978-1-339-01766-2

10 9 8 7 6 5 4 3 2 1   24 25 26 27 28

Printed in the U.S.A.   40

First printing 2024

Book design by Salena Mahina and Two Red Shoes Design

Scholastic Inc.

Meow, meow, meow! You know what that sound means . . . There's a new Dollhouse Delivery!

Gabby looks at the leafy green Kitty Cat Surprise Box. "I feel a gardening theme coming on," she says.

Inside the box is a little potted tree with teeny-tiny cupcakes growing on it!

"Hmmm . . . I wonder if we can eat them," Gabby says. "Maybe Cakey Cat would know! Come on, Pandy. Time to get tiny!"

Gabby and Pandy Paws land in the dollhouse kitchen.

"Hi, Gabby! Hi, Pandy Paws! What's cooking?" Cakey says. He jumps onto the table to greet them. "Oh, you have a Cupcake Tree!"

Pandy Paws giggles. "The cupcakes are so small! I could eat this whole tree by myself!"

"The tree is little now," Cakey says. "But if you give it food, it will grow to full-size with big yummy cupcakes to eat!"

Pandy Paws and Gabby get excited! "What does a Cupcake Tree like to eat?" Gabby asks.

"Honey!" Cakey tells them. "But just a few drops or it'll grow way too big."

After giving the Cupcake Tree a few drops of honey, they find a nice sunny spot for the plant.

"Now," Cakey says, "we wait!"

"But waiting is so hard," Pandy Paws says.

"I know, Pandy. We do hard things all the time," Gabby tells him. "We can't eat the cupcakes yet, but it'll be worth the wait!"

Cakey adds, "I know another cat-tastic snack we can have while we wait!"

While Cakey shows them how to make the new snack, CatRat appears. But Gabby, Pandy, and Cakey don't see him.

"Waiting is for regular cats," he says to himself. "I need a yummy cupcake now!" He pours a bunch of honey into the pot to speed up the growing process.

Whoa! The Cupcake Tree grows right up out of the dollhouse . . . and takes CatRat with it!

CatRat calls his friends for help. "Oh rats! They can't hear me," he says from the tippy-top of the tree.

Back in the kitchen, Gabby, Pandy, and Cakey are surprised to see the Cupcake Tree grow so big. They head outside to get a better look.

"What do we do now?" Pandy asks. "Cakey, you're the cupcake expert. Do you know how to shrink the Cupcake Tree?"

"I have our solution right here! These are Shrinky Sprinkies," Cakey replies. "If we can reach that tippy-top blue cupcake and shake some of these on it, the Cupcake Tree will shrink back down to its regular size!"

They think about this for a moment, then Gabby says, "Let's give it a go!" They start climbing.

They climb up farther. It's grown right through the music room.

"Over here!" DJ Catnip calls from the top of the vine. "I have a situation . . . this giant pink cupcake won't let me go!"

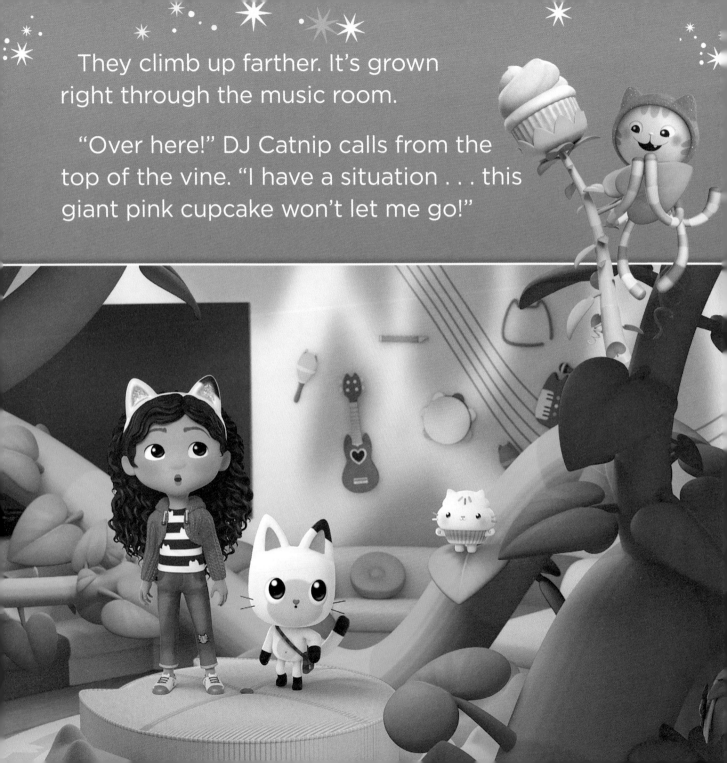

Cakey knows just how to help. "Pink cupcakes love music. If we sing a song, it will shrink back and let go!"

"Let's get on that tune then, kitties!" DJ Catnip cheers.

The song works! They shrink the vine!

The friends are celebrating when they hear someone say, "A little help up here!"

It sounds like Pillow Cat! Gabby, Pandy Paws, and Cakey climb the vine up to the bedroom, but where's Pillow Cat?

"I'm up here!" Pillow Cat says. "I was taking a little catnap, and I woke up stuck in this vine!"

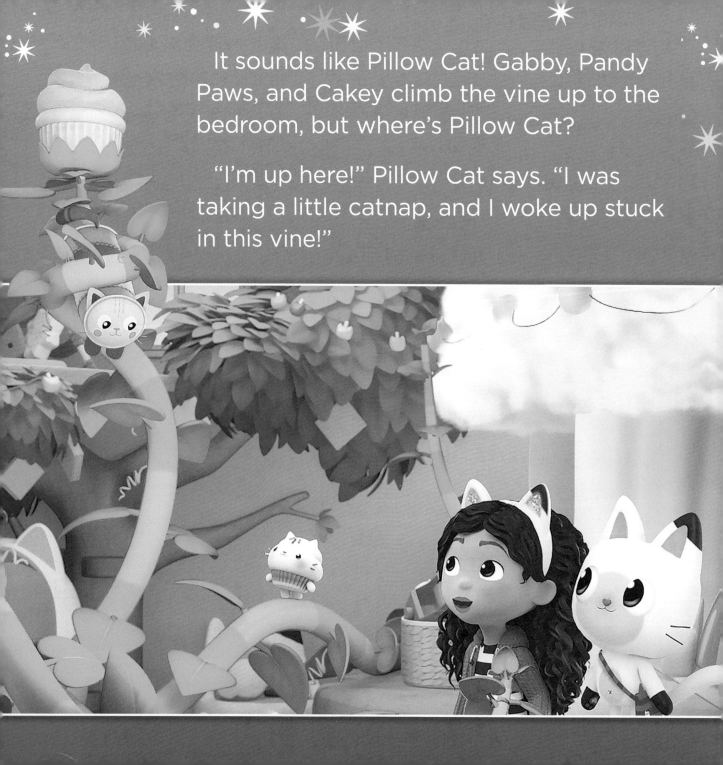

"Cakey, how can we help bring Pillow Cat down to the floor?" Pandy Paws asks.

Cakey says, "Yellow cupcakes love silly stories!"

Pillow Cat tells everyone a story, and they act it out. Just like that, the yellow cupcake shrinks, too!

Then someone says, "Beep, beep! Gabby! Pandy! Help me!"

It's Carlita! Time to climb up the vine to the playroom.

"Carlita, we can hear you, but we can't see you!" Gabby says.

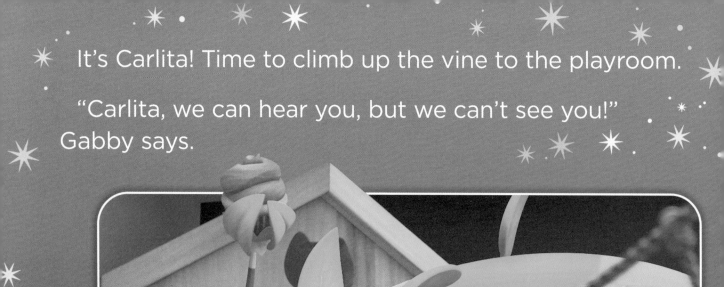

"That's because I'm hiding!" Carlita replies.

"That's right," Cakey says. "Lavender cupcakes love to play hide-and-seek."

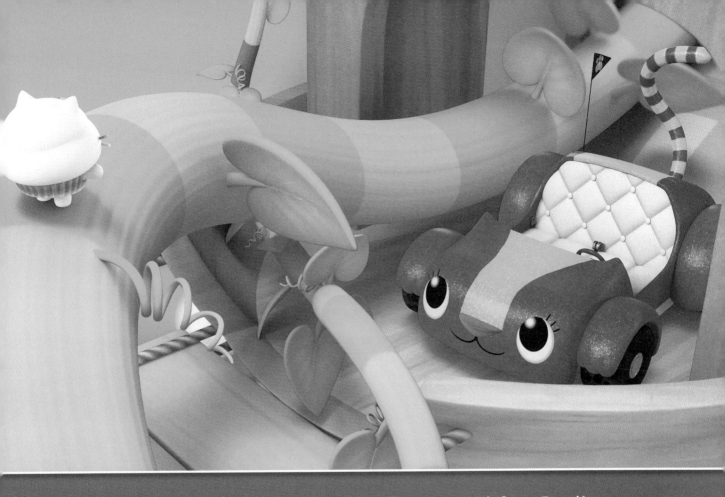

Gabby, Pandy, and Cakey look around for Carlita. Where could she be? Finally, Cakey climbs a big vine and giggles. "We found you!"

"Beep, beep! You sure did!" Carlita says. "Need a ride up to the blue cupcake?"

They all reply together, "Yes!"

Carlita drops them off near the top.

Pandy Paws looks up. "Wow! That's the biggest cupcake of them all!"

Suddenly, someone looks down over the edge. It's CatRat!

He says, "Gabby! Pandy! What took you so long?"

"CatRat! What are you doing up there?" Gabby asks.

CatRat tells them he gave the Cupcake Tree all the honey.

"Don't worry, CatRat, Cakey knows how to get you out of there," Pandy Paws says.

Gabby and Pandy Paws catapult Cakey up to CatRat to use the Shrinky Sprinkies.

It's a Shrinky Sprinkies party!

The Cupcake Tree begins shrinking!

"Yay!" Gabby celebrates. "It's working! A-meow-zing!"

It's Cupcake Time! Everyone picks a cupcake off the tree.

What a paw-sitively delicious day in the dollhouse!